The Secrets of the Stone

Dan Metcalf

ILLUSTRATED BY

Rachelle Panagarry

A & C BLACK
AN IMPRINT OF BLOOMSBURY
LONDON OXFORD NEW DELHI NEW YORK SYDNEY

To Charlie & Isaac.

First published 2015 by
A & C Black, an imprint of Bloomsbury Publishing Plc
50 Bedford Square, London, WC1B 3DP

www.bloomsbury.com

A CIP catalogue for this book is available from the British Library

ISBN 978 1 4729 1184 1

Printed and bound by CPI Group (UK) Ltd, Croydon CR0 4YY

1 3 5 7 9 10 8 6 4 2

Contents

Chapter One

London, 1928

BANG!

Lottie jumped at the noise, almost spilling her cocoa on her cardigan and skirt. The sound echoed off the walls of the museum library's reading room where she was reading her favourite magazine, *True Mysteries.* The story was about

Detective Inspector Victor Blade of Scotland Yard who was hot on the trail of a local burglar called Bloomsbury Bill. Lottie loved to read about DI Blade and couldn't decide whether to be a detective when she grew up, or an archaeologist like her parents. *Maybe both*, she thought.

Lottie climbed out of her special reading nook, looking for the source of the bang. *It looks like I've got a mystery of my own to solve,* she thought.

Lottie had lived in the British Museum since she was four, when her archaeologist parents were killed on a dig in Egypt. The museum was a huge building packed with

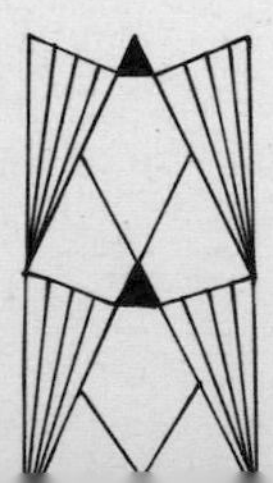

precious artefacts from thousands of years of world history. It was dark now. The winter sun had set and the museum was closed to the public. Lottie left the library and peered down the dark corridor. Where had that noise come from?

"Urrgghhh..."

Lottie froze as she heard a low, deep moan coming from the South American section. She grabbed a nearby pole that they used for opening high windows and tiptoed closer to where the noise was coming from, holding the pole like a weapon. *Just in case,* she thought.

"Urrrrgggghhhhh!"

There it was again! With a deep breath, she pushed the door open with her foot and leapt out into the room. She raised the pole above her head like a spear, ready to strike.

"Lottie?"

Lottie turned on the lights to discover a large man in a linen suit and bow tie lying on the floor.

"Uncle Bert?"

Lottie's Great Uncle, Professor Bertram West, the Curator of Egyptology at the British Museum, was lying flat on his back and grimacing.

The door opened again and Reg, the museum's kindly old caretaker entered.

He was holding his trusty mop, which was about as thin as he was.

"Evening all!" he said cheerily. "'Ello Professor West. What are you doing down there then?"

"I fell," said Uncle Bert. "Your dratted floor is too slippery!"

"Just polished her tonight, with my own special mixture," Reg grinned proudly. "Brings the floorboards up a treat, it does."

"Far too much! I could've been killed!"

The two old men bickered as Lottie played at sliding along Reg's wonderfully polished floor. She had long

ago learned that the trick was to kick off your shoes and run at full speed. She could slide the whole length of the room if she just wore her socks.

"Lottie my dear," said Uncle Bert. "Why do you have that large pole?"

"I thought you might have been a burglar."

"A burglar! The very thought. This is one of the most secure buildings in Britain. No robber would ever dare to break into this old place!"

Lottie shrugged.

"Shame. I'd quite like an adventure."

The two old men continued to bicker about

the polished floor as they all made their way to their rooms to go to bed.

CRASH!

The sound of a window smashing and glass shattering on the floor made the three of them stop dead in their tracks.

"Lottie my dear," said Uncle Bert. "I fear we may yet have that adventure you wished for."

They walked briskly to the source of the noise and found a side window broken. Below it were some muddy footprints

"A clue!" smiled Lottie.

Lottie noted it down in her trusty detective's notebook and the three of them followed the footprints through the museum.

The thief must have been fast, just a few minutes in front of them. The footprints led them toward a vast main hall and Lottie knew precisely where they would stop. Having grown up in the museum, she knew the layout better than anyone and often boasted that she could navigate it blindfolded (she tried it once, but came very close to knocking over an ancient Roman vase. She didn't try it again). The main exhibit in the hall was –

"The Rosetta Stone!" gasped Uncle Bert.

In the centre of the room was a large black rock on a plinth, covered in three different types of white writing. The rope barrier around it had been knocked over. The stone

seemed unharmed, but Uncle Bert ran towards it and fussed over it like it was a toddler who had fallen over in the street.

"There, there," he whispered soothingly. Reg and Lottie exchanged a glance and then burst out laughing.

"You big softie," said Reg. "It's not hurt, it's a rock! Never understood what's so special about it anyway."

Lottie knew all about the stone, having heard the tour guides talk about it.

"It has the same message in three different types of writing engraved on it; Egyptian hieroglyphs, Demotic and ancient Greek. Experts were able to use it to learn to read

hieroglyphs. So the stone is a great big code breaker, unlocking the world of the ancient Egyptians."

"Right," said Reg. "So it's pretty important then?"

"That's putting it mildly," said Uncle Bert. "Lottie my dear, can you put the rope barrier back up please?"

Lottie bent over to retrieve the rope from the floor and noticed something on the stone. She lowered herself down and lay on her back, looking up at the side of the stone.

"There's a secret message written on here! The thief must have known exactly where to look and how to reveal it. They've uncovered

a message which was once painted on to the stone. Now if I can just catch the light at the correct angle..."

"The Trident of Neptune," said Uncle Bert in a whisper. He stood with his eyes wide. Reg and Lottie exchanged confused glances.

"Pardon?" they said.

"A mythical object, belonging to a Roman God. It was lost and stories passed down over the centuries claim that clues are etched on other important artefacts, pointing the way to its resting place."

"Like a treasure hunt," said Lottie.

"Or a wild goose chase," mumbled Reg.

Just then, the three investigators were

startled by a bright light being shone in their eyes. A figure holding a torch approached and Lottie saw the face of Sir Trevelyan Taylor, the Head Curator of the museum. He was a serious man and for some reason he had taken an instant dislike to Lottie and Uncle Bert. He hated them living in the museum.

"I should have known it would be you three. I was passing and saw the lights on. What are you playing at?"

Uncle Bert explained about the break-in and the myth of the Trident of Neptune. Sir Trevelyan scoffed at him.

"Really Bertram, you're losing it. Archaeology is about hard work, not riddles and treasure hunts. Do you really think the Trident of Neptune exists?"

"I'd be prepared to bet my reputation on it," said Uncle Bert proudly.

"You don't have a reputation, except for poor taste in bow ties. But perhaps..." said Sir Trevelyan, his eyes twinkling. "I'll make you a bet. You get the Trident for the museum by tomorrow and I'll double your pay. If you don't get it, you're fired."

Lottie gasped. Uncle Bert would be a fool to agree to a bet like that.

"Deal!" said Uncle Bert. Before she could

stop him, he was shaking Sir Trevelyan's hand.

"You have until midday tomorrow then," said Sir Trevelyan, walking off with a smirk on his face.

"What did you do that for?" said Reg.

"I couldn't help it. He insulted my reputation. No matter, we'll find the Trident, I'm sure of it. What does the message say?" said Uncle Bert.

Lottie crawled back down and quickly scribbled the hidden message onto her detective's notebook:

The Queen resides by the mighty flow,
With apparatus to make it sew.
From ancient lands, leave no stone unturned,
You'll find your prize when it has been earned.

"Crikey!" said Reg. "That's trickier than the weekend crossword. What's it mean then?"

"It means that we need to solve the riddle before the thief cracks it and he's got a head start," said Uncle Bert.

"Then what are we waiting for gentlemen?" said Lottie, hitching up her socks, ready for anything. "Let's get cracking!"

They stared blankly at the riddle on Lottie's notebook for a few moments. Nobody said a word.

"Come on, it can't be that hard!" said Lottie. She began to pace up and down the hall, as she sometimes did when she wanted to think. Reg and Uncle Bert copied her, like a strange game of follow-my-leader. "Let's take it step-by-step."

"Alright," said Uncle Bert. "'*The Queen resides by the mighty flow*'. I suppose the '*mighty flow*' could mean a river."

"Well that's wrong for a start," said Reg. "The Royal Family lives in Buckingham Palace. That's nowhere near the river."

"Hmm," said Lottie, pondering. "'*With apparatus to make it sew*'. They've spelt 'so' wrong. They've put 'sew', like you do with a needle and thread." Lottie stopped pacing, causing Reg and Uncle Bert to crash into each other behind her. "Needle! That's a sewing apparatus. And it doesn't mean *our* Queen. It means an old Queen, like Cleopatra."

Uncle Bert was excited now, almost jumping up and down on the spot.

"'*From ancient lands, leave no stone unturned*'. Of course! It means Cleopatra's Needle. It's a large stone monument that sits on the riverside in London."

Reg looked confused.

"So what does '*You'll find your prize when it has been earned*' mean?"

"I think it means we've got a lot of work to do before we get our hands on that Trident," said Lottie. "So we'd better get a move on. Let's go!"

Chapter Two

Lottie quickly grabbed her coat and hat. She put on her shoes, which were really far too big for her (Uncle Bert always bought her shoes a size too big so she would grow into them). Together with Reg and Uncle Bert, they clambered into the only transport they possessed. Reg's car was old and seemed to be made from four ripped leather seats bound together with rusty metal. Lottie sat in the back of the convertible car in the freezing night air, bouncing up and down as Reg hit every bump and curve in the road.

"Reg, where did you learn to drive?" she shouted from the back seat.

"A bloke down the pub taught me! Not bad eh?"

Lottie gulped. "What do you mean, he 'taught you'?"

"Well, he sort of described what to do and I worked out the rest."

Lottie grabbed hold of the door handle and hoped that they were nearly there.

As they pulled around a corner, she saw

RPI 904

something out of the corner of her eye. Another car, at this time of night? The streets were deserted (just as well, with Reg at the wheel), but a strange black car seemed to be…following them? Lottie shook her head at the silly notion, telling herself off for letting her imagination run away with her.

Cleopatra's Needle was situated next to the River Thames, set on top of a plinth, which described how it had come to be there. To each side was a grand sculpture of an Egyptian sphinx, while the needle itself sat in the middle. A giant stone obelisk, it weighed 224 tons. There were hieroglyphs carved

into each side of the needle and the whole thing looked mightily impressive in the moonlight as Reg pulled up beside it. As they got out of the car, Uncle Bert looked quite ill.

"Are you alright Professor?" said Reg.

"Can I make a request?" said Uncle Bert. "On the way back, can Lottie drive? She can't be any worse a driver than you."

Reg laughed and slapped Uncle Bert on the back.

"I'll ignore that. Crikey!" he said, seeing the needle for the first time. "That thing looks older than me!"

Lottie skipped up to its base.

"It's nearly 3,500 years old, which means it was actually built one thousand years before Cleopatra was born."

They all peered up at the needle, which was covered in markings. If they were looking for a clue, it was well hidden.

"How do we know if the thief has been here already?" said Reg.

"We don't, but they had a head start, so they've probably been and gone. We're playing catch up."

Lottie circled the needle a few times. *How do you hide a clue to find a legendary object? And if the needle has been around for thousands of years, why has no one else ever found the clue*

before? she thought to herself. She looked over to Reg and Uncle Bert, who stared up into the night sky.

"I'll begin to decipher the hieroglyphs on its side," said Uncle Bert with a sigh. "But I warn you, my Egyptian isn't what it used to be, so it may take a while. Reg, be a good chap and shine the headlights over here, will you?"

Reg leapt up to the car and manoeuvred it so that the headlights shone onto the needle. Lottie sat on a step while Uncle Bert got to work. To pass the time, she read a small sign, which was situated close to the base of the obelisk:

CLEOPATRA'S NEEDLE IS A MAJOR BRITISH HISTORICAL LANDMARK. IT WAS GIVEN BY MUHAMMED ALI, RULER OF EGYPT, TO PAY TRIBUTE TO THE BATTLE OF THE NILE, WHERE LORD HORATIO NELSON TRIUMPHED. IT WAS TOWED HERE IN A SPECIAL CONTAINER, BUT ALMOST SANK IN THE BAY OF BISCAY IN 1877.

As she read it, she saw that the headlight's rays caused a reflection on some of the letters on the plaque, as if someone had used clear paint to underline the letters. Lottie tingled with excitement as she realised that this may be the clue they were looking for. She pulled out her detective's notebook and began to note down the message.

◈

"Got it!" called Lottie with satisfaction, after a few minutes of staring at the plaque.

"Got what?" said Reg.

He was standing at the base of Cleopatra's Needle, with Uncle Bert balancing uneasily on his shoulders. Uncle Bert was leaning against the obelisk and copying down the hieroglyphs in his own notebook.

"The next clue!"

"Where?" Reg started to walk over to her, making Uncle Bert wobble on his shoulders. They tottered about for a few seconds, before both falling to the floor in a heap, Reg breaking Uncle Bert's fall.

After some moans of pain and a lot of bickering, Uncle Bert took the notebook from Lottie.

"It was in plain sight the whole time!" said Lottie.

"*Now* you tell us," said Uncle Bert, looking at the piece of paper. It read:

CLIMB HIGH TO THE
BELL IN THE SKY

"Why can't the clues be easier?" moaned Reg. "Something like 'Go back home, I've hidden the treasure under the doormat for you'?"

"I think I know what it means," said Lottie, but the two old men didn't hear her. They were too busy guessing about the clue's meaning for themselves.

"Perhaps it means something about constellations? Stars in the sky?" said Uncle Bert.

"No, I think it means – " Lottie said, trying to get their attention.

"Or maybe a church?"

"No, I think it's – "

They were all interrupted by a loud noise.

Bong! Bong! Bong!

They jumped and span around to look down the river. The Houses of Parliament were silhouetted against the night sky. The clock rang midnight.

"Are you two going to listen to me?" asked Lottie, wild eyed. "A bell in the sky could be – "

"By Jove! That's it!" said Uncle Bert. "Big Ben!"

"That's what I was saying!" yelled Lottie, jumping up and down. Reg and Uncle Bert stared at her, shocked.

"Goodness me Lottie, if you have something to say, just spit it out. You know we'll always listen," said Uncle Bert. Lottie grunted in frustration.

"Never mind! The night's drawing on fast. We only have twelve hours and the thief could have the Trident already. Somehow we've got to get to Big Ben." Lottie pocketed her notebook and leapt up the steps and into the car. "Come on, let's get moving!"

Chapter Three

After another hair-raising journey in the midnight air, they pulled up to the Houses of Parliament in the heart of Westminster. Although it was the middle of the night, Reg was confident that they would be able to get into the grand clock tower that rose 316 feet high above them.

"I know the caretaker, Jim."

"Do all caretakers in London know each

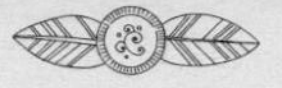

other?" asked Lottie as they got out of the car and walked briskly across to a small door set into the door of Westminster Palace.

"Mostly. We play poker together every Tuesday. Jim here owes me a favour," said Reg. "And a few hundred quid, come to that."

They hammered on the door and Jim, a bleary-eyed small man with a moustache, opened it. Reg started to explain that they needed to get in, but poor Jim was falling asleep on the spot. He let them in and went back to bed, neither knowing nor caring why they wanted to climb the clock tower in the middle of the night. So Lottie, Reg and Uncle Bert found themselves tiptoeing

around the darkened corridors of the Houses of Parliament without a guide.

Inside, it was cold, echoey and a little bit spooky. The only light came from a small oil lamp that Jim had given them, so the shadows on the walls were large and exaggerated. After a few wrong turns, they finally came to a door and Reg paused.

"Here we go. I hope you've got a head for heights!"

They entered and looked up to see a staircase which led up and up and up to the top of the clock tower.

“We’d better get a move on,” said Lottie. “The thief might be close to the Trident already.”

And so they started to climb the 334 steps to the belfry. As they got closer to the top, they could hear the tick, tick, tick of the grand clock, reminding them that time was of the essence. Lottie's legs started to ache halfway up and Uncle Bert looked breathless after only a few minutes. Reg didn't seem to notice the effort, his tall frame almost leaping up the steps.

"How will we know where the clue is?" asked Lottie.

"I suppose we'll see it when we see it," puffed Uncle Bert. "The clue talks about the bell. Did you know that the name 'Big Ben' is the name of the bell, not the tower or the clock?"

They reached the top of the

stairs and came to the platform on which the clock stood. Lottie had never seen anything like it! The workings of the clock lay all about them, cogs and pendulums moving with loud clicks, ticks and tocks. These moved the arms on the clock faces, which were on the four sides of the tower, made from delicate milky white glass panes. Lottie couldn't get over the size of them. One glass panel was missing, so Lottie peered through and saw London in the night time. She saw a huge city lit by streetlights, which looked like tiny pinpricks of white on a black canvas. The only thing she couldn't see was the clock tower, which was directly below her.

"There's the beauty!" said Reg. Looking up they could see the undersides of the bells that struck the hour. There were four smaller ones and one large one with a crack in it – this was Big Ben.

Lottie searched the belfry for clues, hoping to find a simple note or a riddle, but they couldn't find anything.

"This is hopeless!" she cried. She inwardly told herself off after saying it. Would DI Blade give up? Of course not! He'd carry on through the night until the thief was in his grasp. Lottie looked again at the great bell. She noticed that around the rim of it were markings that she recognised.

"Found it!" she sang. Uncle Bert and Reg gathered around. Stamped into the rim of the bell were a series of dots and dashes. Lottie noted the code down in her detective's notebook:

.- / --. .-. . . -.- / ... . --- . /
... . - / .. -. / ... - --- -. .

"It doesn't look like much of a code to me," said Reg.

"It's Morse Code," said Lottie. "It's usually used to send codes electronically over a telegraph wire. I read about it in my *True Mysteries* magazine."

"It makes sense," said Uncle Bert. "Morse Code was invented in the 1840s, about the same time that the Houses of Parliament were being built. They must have built the code into the bell when it was being cast. Ingenious!"

Lottie flipped through her notebook, where she had a cutting from her *True Mysteries* magazine. It was the key to the code.

MORSE CODE

A	•—	M	——	Y	—•——
B	—•••	N	—•	Z	——••
C	—•—•	O	———	0	—————
D	—••	P	•——•	1	•————
E	•	Q	——•—	2	••———
F	••—•	R	•—•	3	•••——
G	——•	S	•••	4	••••—
H	••••	T	—	5	•••••
I	••	U	••—	6	—••••
J	•———	V	•••—	7	——•••
K	—•—	W	•——	8	———••
L	•—••	X	—••—	9	————•

"I knew this would come in handy one day!" she smiled.

"Now all we have to do is match up the letters and we'll have our clue!"

She looked proudly at her friends. They looked blankly back.

"Get on with it then! I want to get back to my bed!" said Reg.

Lottie sighed and set about cracking the code.

Lottie scribbled the answer as fast as she could.

"There!" she said. She showed them the notebook.

.- / --. .-. . . -.- / ... . --- . /

... . - / .. -. / ... - --- -. .

A / GREEK / SHOE / SET / IN / STONE

They all stared at the clue for a while longer.

"No, it means nothing to me," said Uncle Bert after a few tense moments.

“Nor me,” sighed Lottie. She sat down on the floor and put her head in her hands. Uncle Bert joined her.

“Really?” said Reg. “It seems pretty obvious to me.” Lottie and Uncle Bert looked back up at him, both frowning. “Don’t look at me like that! I know I ain’t got much in the old brainbox department, but you don’t work in a museum all of your life without picking up a few bits of information here and there.”

Lottie jumped up, excited once more. “Go on then!”

Reg smiled proudly.

"Is this what it feels like to be the clever one?" he said, toying with his friends.

"Get on with it!" they both shouted.

"Alright! So we're looking for a Greek shoe, set in stone. That could be a statue of some sort. The most famous Greek ones I know of are the Elgin Marbles."

"Which are back in the museum! Reginald my boy, you're brilliant!" said Uncle Bert as he stood up to join them. He shook the old caretaker's hand with glee.

From underneath them came a slow hand clap. Up the steps came a man, all dressed in black, but with a shock of curly white hair.

"Bravo," he said with no emotion and an unexpected posh accent. "You really are quite the team."

"Who the devil are you?" asked Uncle Bert.

"You may well ask, Professor West," said the man. "Allow me to introduce myself. My friends call me Bill and you've just led me to my fortune."

Lottie gasped.

"You're Bloomsbury Bill from my crime magazines! You broke into the museum!"

"Precisely," he said. "I've been researching the Trident of Neptune for some time and tonight I finally uncovered a clue on the Rosetta Stone. When you came along and

solved it, I thought I'd tag along to see how far you got."

Lottie thought back.

"You were in the black car!" she said, furious with herself for not taking the earlier sighting seriously. "So all the time we thought we were chasing you – "

"*I* was following *you*. Yes." He smiled. It looked horrible, like a snake digesting its meal. "And you will now lead me to the Trident."

"Oh really? And what makes you think we'll do that?" said Reg, raising himself up for a fight.

"This," said Bloomsbury Bill. His hand

suddenly held a small gun. He pointed it at the three of them.

"Ooh, hecky thump," said Reg with a gulp.

Chapter Four

They drove carefully back to the museum. Bloomsbury Bill joined them, his gun trained on them all the way. Once they arrived they got out of the car and walked to the Greek section, deep in the heart of the museum, where the Elgin Marbles were on display. Lottie whispered to Uncle Bert as they walked side by side.

"We can't let him have the Trident, Uncle Bert!" hissed Lottie.

"He's got a gun!"

"He's a thief and a bully! And he doesn't deserve it. We did all the work."

"Lottie darling, just do as he says. I don't want you to get hurt."

They came to the correct room and Reg flicked the lights on as he walked in, illuminating the marbles. They were huge sculptures of Greek gods in smooth white stone.

"Here we are," said Uncle Bert. "Now what?"

"We hunt for the Trident of course," said Bill. He strolled up and down the room admiring the sculptures. "They really are quite beautiful aren't they? Did you know that the temple that they came from was built around 2,500 years ago in Greece? When an army used the temple as a gunpowder store in the seventeenth century, there was a huge explosion, destroying the building completely. Lord Elgin transferred the surviving sculptures here in the early 1800s."

Uncle Bert stared at the burglar in disbelief.

"You know, you're remarkably well educated for a common thief."

"Less of the 'common', if you please," Bloomsbury Bill laughed. "I had a good reputation once. Now I find that stealing is easier than working and so much more fun! Now come along, get searching. Remember, we're looking for a 'Greek shoe'."

Lottie begrudgingly looked for the clues. The marbles were mostly friezes, large white marble slabs with figures sculpted into them. There were other figures, which would have stood atop the entrance of the temple. These were gods and goddesses, wearing togas or nothing at all. Over the years, some

of the figures had lost their feet altogether, having had them blown off in an explosion or knocked off by careless passers-by. The figures that remained were mostly barefoot. It *was* ancient Greece after all. Lottie suspected they didn't wear a nice pair of leather boots around Athens in 500 BC.

She looked around and saw the others were looking blank also. The room they were in was large and she was now a good distance from Bloomsbury Bill. Maybe she could get away and raise the alarm, if only…

Just then, her eye caught a different sort of sculpture; an army of soldiers and horses, which got her thinking.

Horses wore shoes, didn't they?

She searched the exhibit with a renewed energy and came across one horse with its hooves showing a definite horseshoe pattern on the bottom. She vaguely remembered from one of the books she had read in the library (or perhaps it was Uncle Bert boring her with another piece of seemingly useless information), that horseshoes didn't come into common use until 1000 AD, meaning they were totally out of place on this sculpture. Maybe whoever had set the trail had added the horseshoe themselves with a hammer and chisel. She ducked under the red rope barrier to take a closer look. Sure enough,

she could see a small message imprinted on the bottom of the shoe:

180 ACW

She glanced over at Bloomsbury Bill, who wasn't paying any attention to her. He probably thought she was just an annoying

little girl who was up past her bedtime. Well she'd show him! If she could just work out what she had to do, she could get away and keep the Trident for herself. Uncle Bert would keep his job, winning his foolish bet.

She stared at the secret message on the sculpture and concentrated.

Lottie bit her lip as she concentrated and the answer hit her. Thank goodness she had paid attention in Uncle Bert's maths lessons. ACW must stand for anti-clockwise and 180 must be the amount of degrees – a half turn!

She checked that Bloomsbury Bill wasn't looking and reached out to the horseshoe. She grabbed it and turned, surprised to find that it slid easily around to face the other way like a key in a lock. She smiled as the horseshoe clicked into position and she felt the stone panel behind it shift, exposing a crack in the sculpture.

At first she thought she had broken it, but

Lottie stepped back and saw that the crack was actually the start of a door. Checking over her shoulder again, she gave the frieze a nudge. It slid open like a freshly oiled door. Lottie's heart leapt as it revealed a shining silver trident, a giant weapon with three prongs at the top.

"Found something?" said Bloomsbury Bill. He was at the other end of the long room and Lottie knew that she would have to act fast.

"There's no way I'm letting a bully like him take this away from us," she whispered to herself.

Without thinking, she grabbed the Trident

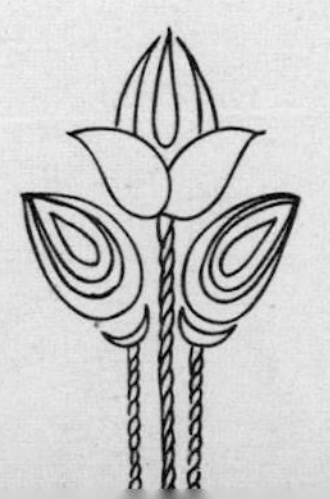

of Neptune from the secret compartment and ran as fast as she could to the nearest exit.

"Get back here you little thief!" shouted Bloomsbury Bill. Lottie thought that was a bit rich, coming from him. He had anger in his voice and immediately gave chase. Lottie was already through the door, but she could hear his heavy footsteps as he pounded through the corridors. She sped around a corner, the Trident heavy in her hands, but her pulse was racing so fast that it gave her energy and strength.

"I'll tear you limb from limb, you greasy little tyke!" threatened Bloomsbury Bill, his voice echoing in the empty, dark museum.

Lottie didn't dare look back. Thank goodness she knew the halls and corridors so well. Even if Bloomsbury Bill caught up with her, she knew all the best places to hide.

She turned the corner and stopped dead. Bloomsbury Bill stood in front of her, grinning menacingly.

"You're not the only one who knows a few shortcuts kid," he said, stepping closer. "I studied this museum for months trying to find that trident. Now give it here."

Lottie forced herself to show no fear.

"Come and get it!" she shouted and ran off in the opposite direction. Bloomsbury Bill was hot on her heels now, just a few paces behind

her. She had lost her head start, but she still had youth and intelligence on her side.

An idea came to her.

She allowed her shoes to slip off as she turned into a corridor. She sped up and ran full pelt. Just when she could run no faster, she stopped and slid across the wooden floor at an impressive speed, just as she had planned.

Behind her, Bloomsbury Bill turned and accelerated also, but hadn't noticed Reg's super-shiney-slidey waxed floor.

He screamed as he lost his footing and seemed to hang in mid-air for a second or two. His legs kicked desperately, trying to get a grip on the floor, but he fell flat on his back, knocking himself out cold. Lottie made her way back to where he was lying and stood over him proudly.

"That's what you get for bullying Lottie Lipton!" she said triumphantly.

Chapter Five

"I have to say Professor West, when someone rang Scotland Yard and said they'd captured Bloomsbury Bill all on their own, I thought it was a wind-up."

Detective Inspector Victor Blade stood in the courtyard of the British Museum dressed in his usual attire of a raincoat and three-piece-suit. Two uniformed police

officers led Bloomsbury Bill across the large space in handcuffs. "Yet here he is. Keep an eye on him lads," he called to the policemen. "He's a slippery little beggar."

It was early morning and the sun was coming up over the rooftops of London. Uncle Bert stood in the courtyard too, yawning widely.

"I'm afraid I can claim none of the credit, Detective Inspector," he said. He went on to recount the entire adventure, while the policeman made notes in his trusty notebook.

"What a marvellous story," said Blade finally. "I'd like to meet this niece of yours."

They went indoors where Lottie and Reg, too excited to sleep, sat on some steps playing cards.

"Lottie? There's someone here who wants to meet you."

Lottie jumped up and recognised him immediately. She was too amazed to speak, her voice disappearing.

"That was pretty good work you did tonight," said Blade. "Usually I'd say to never take on a criminal yourself. It can be a dangerous business and we wouldn't want anyone to get hurt. In this case however, I think I should be telling criminals not to mess with Lottie Lipton!"

TRUE
MYSTERIES

They all laughed. Lottie could not believe her hero was standing right in front of her.

"C-can you sign this please?" she said, finding her voice. She handed him a copy of *True Mysteries* magazine, which he signed with a flourish.

"I'd better be off," he said. He winked at Lottie as he left.

"That was some night," said Reg with a tired stretch.

"Uh-oh," said Uncle Bert. "Looks like it isn't over yet." He nodded at the entrance, where Sir Trevelyan Taylor was barging through the doors.

"Bertram!" he bellowed. "What's the meaning of this? There's police everywhere!"

"Calm down Sir Trev. We've had a busy night, that's all," said Reg.

"Busy? If my museum is damaged in any way, I'll – " He fell silent as Uncle Bert produced the glittering silver Trident of Neptune and laid it in his hands.

"Yours, I believe?" said Lottie.

"B-but … I … H-how … ?" stuttered Sir Trevelyan. He had turned a pleasing shade of pink.

"I'll expect my new *double* pay at the end of the month," said Uncle Bert with a grin. "Anyone for cocoa?"

Reg and Uncle Bert strolled off, already bickering about the best way to make cocoa.

Lottie patted Sir Trevelyan on the arm as she passed, who looked like he was going to faint.

"Yes, that really was some night," she said to herself. She looked down at the magazine in her hands and opened it to look at the inscription.

To Lottie,
Your Uncle tells me that you can't decide whether to be an archaeologist or a detective when you're older. Whatever your decision, you'll be welcome at Scotland Yard in my team.
DI Blade

Cleopatra Queen of Egypt between 44 BC and 30 BC. She was the last Pharaoh (ruler) of ancient Egypt.

Elgin Marbles Large collection of Greek sculptures in the British Museum. They were originally part of the Parthenon, an ancient temple in Athens.

Houses of Parliament The buildings in London where Members of Parliament meet to run the country.

Morse Code A system which uses dots and dashes in place of letters. It was

invented in 1836 by Samuel Morse.

Neptune The Roman God of the Sea. He is often pictured in paintings and mosaics riding a horse and holding a large Trident.

Rosetta Stone A large stone in the British Museum. On it is a law written by King Ptolemy V in three different languages.

Scotland Yard The Police Force in London.

Trident A three-pronged spear used for fishing and in battles.

Did You Know?

- Big Ben weighs 13 tonnes.
- The tower that Big Ben stands in was renamed Elizabeth Tower in 2012 to celebrate the Diamond Jubilee of Queen Elizabeth II.
- Cleopatra lived between 69 BC and 30 BC.
- The ancient Greeks believed in a family of gods and goddesses, with King Zeus as the King of the Gods.

Crack the Code!

Use the Morse Code table from Chapter Three to decipher this message:

.-.. --- - - .. . / .-- .. .-.. .-.. /

.-. . - ..- .-. -. / .. -. /

- .... . / ... -.-. .-. --- .-.. .-.. /

--- ..-. / .- -.. . -..- .- -. -.. .-. .. .-/

--- ..- - / ... --- --- -.!